# The 101 Dalmatians

GALLERY BOOKS
An imprint of W.H. Smith Publishers Inc.
112 Madison Avenue
New York, New York 10016

Hi! My name is Pongo. This is my master, Roger
Radcliffe. He's a musician. You can see that right away.
All he needs to keep him happy is his piano and his
pipe. We get along fine. While he's writing songs, I
think. I've got nothing against having a good dinner, a
few pats on the back from Roger, a short walk and
a cozy basket to sleep in. But, somehow, it's just not
enough. I need to think. And, while he's working, I
think and I think. In fact, that's how this story begins.

It was a sunny spring day. The park in front of the house was full of people walking. I was bored, but Roger was too busy with his music to notice that what we needed was a companion. There were lots to choose from. I used to watch them from the window every day. Miss Poodle? No, too snobby and I was sure Roger would not care for her mistress. That Afghan wasn't too bad, but she looked a bit snooty, and as for her mistress... no, not quite right for Roger.

It's no joke trying to find the other half of a couple. Especially when you're looking for a pair.

Ah!!! now this is better. Look at those two! Perfect! A sleek-looking animal of my own distinguished breed. A Dalmatian. She was so lovely that my heart missed a few beats. And, as for her mistress... not bad at all! Tall, elegant and she's carrying a book. Must be a brainy type... just like Roger.

If only Roger could see her. But he's too busy with his music. They're going away. Quick! I can't let those two get away. How am I going to get Roger's attention?

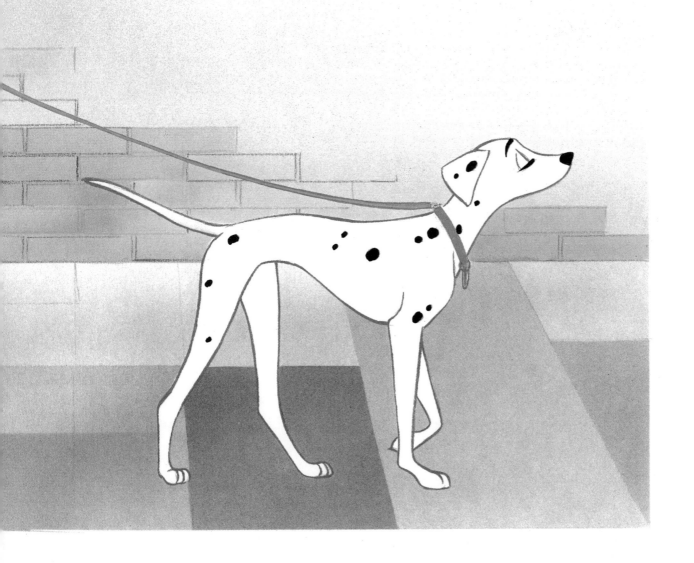

I've got it! I'll just push the clock hand forward with my paw. When Roger sees the time, he'll take me for my daily walk.

Clever idea, don't you think? But unfortunately he's not looking at the clock. He's too busy tinkering away at the piano.

Looks like I'll have to make some noise myself.

"WOOFF WOOFF!" I barked. "Hurry, master, it's time for my walk." I'm not usually so pushy, but this was an emergency.

Roger looked up from the piano. "Time for your walk already? All right, let's go." There was no time to waste. I grabbed his hat and my lead and carried them to him in my mouth.

I was at the door in a flash, my tail wagging like mad.

I spotted them as soon as
we entered the park. But
Roger decided to sit down
beside the pond.

I had to do something. I
grabbed Roger's hat and
carried it over to the lady.
"WOOFF WOOFF! Here's a
present. It's from that man
sitting over there."

Roger wandered over and
started to apologize. "He's a
silly dog. I'm sorry if he's
bothered you."

"Oh no, really it's quite all right," she replied.

Sometimes I wonder about these human beings. They are so slow! While they were busy making small talk, the Dalmatian, Perdita, and I had already decided that this was it. We knew that we were meant for each other. We jumped and danced and ran circles around their legs. Soon our leads became entangled and our humans fell into the pond! Oh no! This was trouble.

Amazingly enough, though, they weren't even angry. In fact, they're laughing. They were soaked from head to toe, but they looked happy. And later...

Well, good old Roger wasn't so slow after all. Before you could blink an eye, he was asking Anita, that's the lady's name, to marry him. Sometimes I guess I don't give human beings enough credit!

But it was really Perdita and I who had done all the work. The house became a paradise for dogs and their masters.

16

Our peace was shattered one day by the simple ring of the doorbell. Anita answered the door, with us at her heels.

In walked a creature wearing a tight satin dress and fur coat.

"Hello darling! Remember me? I'm Cruella de Ville. We went to school together," she said, waving her cigarette and filling the place with smoke. Not only that, but she must have been wearing a gallon of perfume. Phew! This was too much for my delicate nose.

She finally came to the point of her visit. "Anita darling, I believe that Perdita's expecting little ones. And you know how much I just adore puppies. You will keep one for me?"

When she left, Perdita and I looked at Anita. We were thinking about our puppies.

Anita too was thinking about them. I don't think she liked the idea of giving one away to that woman, either. When Roger came home and found us all wearing such sad faces, he decided to cheer us up and began dancing with Anita. And before we knew it, we were all dancing and laughing.

Cruella was forgotten—at least for the time being.

The big day arrived. While
Anita was helping Perdita,
Roger and I waited outside
the door. We were both
pretty nervous. There seemed
to be a lot of noise coming
from behind the door.
Finally Anita came out
wearing a big smile.

Perdita lay on the cushions with a tired smile on her face. Next to her were five... ten... fifteen!!! little white balls of fluff. Wow! Fifteen puppies! I was the proudest father on the block.

Perdita and I were the happiest parents in the world. Roger even composed a special lullaby for the pups. Things just couldn't have been better.

Riinngg! The doorbell rang so loudly that I jumped into Roger's arms. It was Cruella de Ville. She hadn't forgotten us. "I heard that Perdita and Pongo have 15 puppies. It's just wonderful news," she cried. She looked down at the puppies. "How much?" she asked, beginning to write out a check. I started to tremble. But Roger was firm. He told her that none of the puppies were for sale.

Cruella became so mad that she splattered ink all over us.

When Cruella had left, Roger told Anita that there was nothing to worry about. That woman would never get her hands on the puppies.

As the weeks passed, the puppies' spots began to appear. They were a joy to us. They loved to watch the television. Their favorite program was about a dog called Thunder. He was a sheriff's dog in the Wild West.

We used to gather in front
of the television every night.
Some of the puppies would
climb onto the sofa for a
better view. Whenever
Thunder came onto the
screen, the puppies would
bark with excitement.

One of the little ones,
Pepper, stood on my head
and growled at the bandit.
Some of the other pups
became frightened and ran
away to hide under the sofa.

Nanny heard the barking and came into the TV room to investigate. "I think it's time you were all in bed! Come now, sleepy times," she said as she began picking up the pups. Good old Nanny! She was the one who looked after us all. She helped Anita with the cooking and dusted the piano for Roger.

She put all the pups to bed in their basket in the kitchen. "Now, now, Pepper. Time for you to get some sleep," she gently scolded as she tucked him into bed.

It was the hour for our
evening stroll.

Two men were watching
from a truck parked outside
the house. "Okay. There they
go. Now it's time to make
the move," said one as he
saw us walk away.

Nanny answered the door. "Sorry to disturb you Madam, but we've come about the electricity," said the taller one of the two.

"At this time of night?" Nanny exclaimed. "Come back in the morning. And anyway, there's nothing wrong with the electricity," she said, beginning to close the door.

But these men wouldn't take no for an answer. They pushed the door open and went into the house.

"Don't you dare come in here!" shouted Nanny, chasing them into the hall. But they paid no attention.

"Where do you think you're going?" she cried as she grabbed at their coats. The skinny one rushed up the stairs, while the other ran toward the kitchen.

"Oh dear! I wish Master Roger was here," she cried. "What am I to do?"

Soon, the two men found
what they were after. It
wasn't money or jewels.
They were stealing the
puppies! The two of them
stuffed the fifteen pups into
a big bag.

"Let's get out here before
the others come back," said
the big man as they ran out
of the back door.

Hearing the door slam, Nanny rushed into the kitchen. When she saw the puppies' empty basket, she began to cry.

As soon as Roger heard the terrible news he picked up the phone and called the police. "Our fifteen Dalmatian puppies have been stolen. You must help us get them back," Roger explained to the policeman. "I don't know who could have done this. But please, you must find them for us."

The next morning, Cruella de Ville read of the puppies' kidnapping in the newspapers. She was grinning from ear to ear as she picked up the telephone. "Congratulations, boys. You did a good job. I'll be coming in a minute," she said and she put down the phone.

In the meantime, Perdita and I decided to take things into our own hands. We went out to look for our friends—they'd help us.

Danny, the Great Dane, and his sidekick, Scottie, were the first to come running. "Who's been kidnapped?" asked Danny.

"I can't believe it," said Scottie. "Don't worry, we'll tell all the others."

And soon enough the dogs began howling. The message was passed on from dog to dog. What a commotion! With all the noise, no one got much sleep that night!

On the other side of the city, Old Towser and his pal, Lucy the goose, picked up the news. "What's that about 15 puppies?" said Old Towser, who was a bit deaf.

"Someone's stolen Pongo and Perdita's pups," Lucy screeched into his ear.

"Well stop squawking and let's get to work," said Old Towser as he ran to the top of the highest hill in the city.

Old Towser barked the message to all the dogs, while Lucy alerted the other animals.

The news reached a farm where Colonel, the sheepdog, lived. The Colonel and his partner, Tibbs the cat, were famous throughout the animal world. They were a team of ace detectives.

And this was a job for experts!

Captain the horse was the first to pick up the message. He and his buddy Tibbs woke the Colonel.

"There's an urgent message from London. Listen!" All three perked up their ears. "Is it war?" asked Captain, always ready for battle.

"No, it's a kidnapping. Puppies... 15 Dalmatian puppies... last night," said the Colonel.

Tibbs scratched his ear. "Funny. Last night while I was prowling around Hell Hall I heard some yelping. The lights were on and smoke was coming from the chimney."

"Hum!" said the Colonel. "That place has been empty for years! Sounds like something fishy is going on over there. Did you say you heard yelping?"

"Sure sounded like dogs to me," said Tibbs.

"I think this calls for an investigation," said the Colonel. "Come on Tibbs, let's go have a look."

Tibbs jumped on the Colonel's back and off they
trudged through the snow. "Look! Paw prints. Lots of
them," said the Colonel, sniffing the snow near the
deserted mansion.

"And there's a light on—over there in the window,"
whispered Tibbs. Silently, the two detectives crept up
around the side of the abandoned building. When they
reached the window they both looked in and spotted
the Dalmatians.

What a scene! In a sofa sat a sleazy-looking character with a bottle of wine in his hand. Surrounding him were 10... 15... 20... 50 — maybe more — little Dalmatians!

"I thought you said 15 puppies were kidnapped," whispered the Colonel.

"That's right. The message said 15. What are the rest of these puppies doing here?" replied Tibbs.

"You go in and find out what's going on. I'll go back and send a message to Pongo," said the Colonel. He headed back to the farm.

Meanwhile, inside the house the puppies were all gathered in front of the TV. They didn't know where they were nor who the other pups were. But at least there was a TV.

Tibbs found a hole in the wall and crept into the room. "This is crazy," he thought. "How am I ever going to tell which of these puppies belong to Perdita and Pongo? They all look alike to me. And there are so many of them. There must be almost a hundred."

"Psst! You over there. What's going on here?" Tibbs hissed into the ear of one of the puppies. The puppy listened as Tibbs explained about the kidnapping.

"I don't know any Pongo," said the puppy. "A lady bought me and my brothers in London. We've been here for a couple of days. But there were some new puppies that arrived a few hours ago. That's them in front of the television. I think there were fifteen of them."

Tibbs became excited when he heard this. "I must get near the television. But how am I going to get past that man?"

Tibbs tiptoed up to the chair. Just as he was at the top, the man moved. "Maybe if I stay perfectly still, he won't know I'm here," thought Tibbs as he froze beside the wine bottle.

Without looking, the man reached for his wine. He grabbed Tibbs by the neck. "Oh, no! Now I'm in big trouble," thought the cat.

Horace, the robber, didn't realize what he was doing. He was about to take a swig when Tibbs let out an enormous MIIAAOOWW!!! Horace was so stunned that he dropped the cat.

Tibbs shot off like a flash.

Meanwhile, the Colonel had passed on the news. The message traveled back to the city. Farm dogs told house dogs and so on, until Danny, the Great Dane, heard the word. "The puppies have been found—alive and well," he told Perdita and Pongo.

"Where are they?" asked Perdita.

"They are hidden in the deserted mansion near Hell Hole."

"Spread the word. We're coming," barked Pongo as he and Perdita ran off in the direction of their pups.

Back at the mansion, Cruella de Ville was busy counting the puppies. She was thinking of all the lovely coats and hats that their furs would make.

Seeing Horace and Jasper —the kidnappers— in front of the TV, she began to shout. "I'm not paying you guys to watch TV. Get up, you hoodlums! I want those puppies skinned before tomorrow!"

"Okay! Okay! We'll deal with the puppies as soon as the program's over," said Jasper, covering his ears.

Tibbs had heard everything. "This calls for fast action," he thought. "There's no time to wait for the others to come."

"Quick!" he hissed at the puppies. "Follow me and don't make a peep! You're in danger. I've got to get you out of here—now!"

The puppies were frightened and did as they were told, all except Lucky who was busy watching the television. Neither he nor the robbers saw what was happening. Their eyes were glued to the TV.

Tibbs had never worked so hard. It was no joke trying to get all those puppies out without making a sound. Just as he was pushing the last puppy through the hole he heard Lucky barking at the TV.

Rushing back to get him, he saw that the program was over! The robbers had noticed that the puppies were gone. They began swearing and shouting.

At that very same moment
Perdita and Pongo were
nearing the mansion. They
could hear the yelling.
"Hurry!" urged Pongo.
"Something's going on in
there."

Tibbs had grabbed Lucky and led him off with the others. He rushed down the staircase looking for a place to hide. Hundreds of little paws were running as fast as they could. Some of them tumbled over—but not a cry was heard.

Tibbs and the puppies hid under the staircase.
"Shush!" whispered the cat, silencing one of the
puppies with his paw. He heard growling noises.
"Ah! The others have finally arrived!"

There was a terrible howling and screaming as Pongo and Perdita rushed into the mansion and attacked. They were so quick that Horace didn't know what had hit him. Pongo bared his teeth, while Perdita snapped at Horace's coat. "Leave me alone! I swear I didn't do anything," cried Horace as he fell to the ground.

"What have you done with
my puppies?" snarled Perdita.
"Leave this one to me,"
said Pongo. "You take care
of the fat one."

Jasper backed away as Perdita ran toward him. He was trying to reach for the fire poker. Pepper came to give his mother a hand. The two dogs grabbed the corners of the rug and gave it a yank. Wooosh! Boom! Jasper had fallen in front the fire.

"That will keep him out of our way!" cried Perdita as she, Pongo and Pepper ran off to find the puppies.

Sniff! Sniff! Jasper smelled something burning.

"YOW! OUCH!" he screamed, rushing outside, trailing smoke behind him. "This place is haunted," he thought as he sat in the snow.

While Perdita and Pongo were dealing with the crooks, Tibbs had led the puppies to the Colonel's farm. And this is where the two parents found their puppies.

"Look sharp!" ordered the Colonel. "You're not out of danger yet! Those two scoundrels will be here at any minute. Hide in Captain's stable. I'll keep watch!"

Sure enough! No sooner had the dogs hidden behind
the haystacks, when Jasper and Horace arrived on the
scene. The Colonel watched from the doorway.

"Look! More prints," said Horace.

"Yeah! But where are those mutts?" replied Jasper,
who was carrying a big club.

"The tracks lead into the stable. Come on. Let's have
a look. They won't get away this time," said Horace.

The two looked around the stable but found no pups. "You dope" cried Jasper. "I thought you said they were here."

"Well, I saw the prints. They can't be far away," Horace replied.

Tibbs whispered into the horse's ear. "Okay Captain, now it's your turn to have some fun. Ready, steady, go!"

Captain reared his hind legs. BAAMM! Jasper and Horace went whizzing over the Colonel's head. They landed head first in the snow.

Rubbing their sore behinds they stared at the dozens and dozens of pawprints.

Perdita, Pongo and the
puppies had slipped out by
the back of the stable. They
ran with all their might, but
it wasn't easy for the little
ones. Pongo picked the
smallest one up and carried
her in his mouth.

Ahead of them was a farm.
If only they could make it
that far.

The farm dog had come out to meet them. "Look at those little ones," he said to Pongo. "They are exhausted. Spend the night in the barn. You can all rest and get an early start in the morning."

Pongo wanted to keep running. But Perdita spoke up. "He's right. Look at these poor little things. They must have some rest."

Pongo took one look at the shivering, sleepy pups, and had to agree. "Okay. We'll stop for now."

Perdita led the puppies into the barn. Two cows and a bull watched them go by. "My, what a big family you have!" exclaimed the bull.

"If you need any milk, I've plenty!" said his wife, one of the cows.

Soon everyone settled down to sleep. However, the night was short. They were all up and on the run again at dawn.

Perdita and the puppies ran on ahead, while Pongo stayed behind to sweep away their tracks. Soon he heard two cars approaching. It was Cruella de Ville and the two crooks.

"This is your last chance, you numbskulls! Follow me into that village. I want those dogs NOW!!"

Pongo ran to catch up with his family. Perdita and the pups had met a friendly Labrador who was hiding them in an old coal shed.

"In a few minutes the coal truck will be leaving for London. You can ride in the back," he told Pongo.

At that moment, Cruella drove by. She was furious. "Look! She's on our trail. How will we get into the truck without her seeing us?" whispered Pongo.

"Simple," said the Lab. "Roll yourselves in the coal dust. She's looking for dogs with spots. Not black ones."

What a great idea, and so much fun too! Pongo was the first. Then the pups joined in. Soon they were black from head to tail.

Outside there was a sudden screech of brakes. Cruella had found some tracks. She stopped the engine and called out to Jasper and Horace. "Look! Pawprints! I know they are somewhere around here. Go look behind that coal shed. I'll watch from here. You'd better not botch things up this time—or I'll have *your* skins!"

While Cruella was giving her orders, Pongo and the puppies filed toward the waiting truck. Cruella was a bit surprised to see so many black puppies. "I didn't know they raised Labradors in this village," she mumbled as she watched them go by.

Horace turned to look at the dogs. "Wouldn't it be funny if Dalmatians turned themselves into Labradors."

"Sure! That would be some miracle," laughed Jasper.

"Stop babbling like idiots and go find those dogs!" screamed Cruella, whose temper was beginning to flare.

"What!! More Labradors!" she shouted, as Perdita and the last batch of puppies ran past the car. They were almost there... just a few more steps. SPLAATT! Some melting snow had fallen onto Perdita and the pups. Small white spots were beginning to appear on the dogs' backs. Cruella leaned out of the window. Her brain started ticking... "White spots on black dogs... black spots on white dogs! Of course! Those aren't Labradors."

"Why you clever dogs!"
she said. "But not clever
enough! Horace! Jasper! Over
here! Look! I think your
miracle has come true.
Those aren't Labradors
—they're Dalmatians!"
  Cruella de Ville sniggered
with delight.

Perdita and the puppies made a dash for the truck. Pongo was waiting to lift them up. Soon they were all inside. The engine roared as the truck drove off. Just in time! Cruella laughed as she saw the truck drive off. "I'll catch up with that old wreck in no time. This car of mine can run circles around that old heap!"

Cruella stepped on the gas pedal. Her car raced up next to the truck. She was trying to force it off the road. But she didn't see the bridge up ahead. Before she knew it her car had crashed through the railing and was plunging into the ravine.

The car toppled over in the snow, rolling over several times before coming to a halt. Parts of the roof and hood had been lost, but Cruella was still behind the wheel. And she was madder than ever.

Ranting and raving, she clung to the steering wheel as the car raced back up the hill. Nothing was going to prevent her from having her way. Flames burst from the engine as she raced after the truck.

"Oh no! Here she comes again!" cried Perdita. "Please can't you go any faster?" she asked the driver.

"Watch out!" shouted Pongo. "That blue van is heading this way."

But, instead of cutting off the truck, Jasper and Horace slammed right into the side of Cruella's car.

BAANNG! CRAASSHH! Cruella and the two crooks went flying through the air. The race was over. And Cruella de Ville had lost—forever!

Several hours later, Anita let out a shriek as a big black dog came running into her living room. She backed up against the sofa and reached out to push the dog away.

"What's this?" she said as she looked down at her hands. They were black. She rubbed the dog's head. "Why it's Perdita!" she cried with joy. "You've come back! And your puppies—everyone safe and sound," she said as she gave Perdita a big hug.

Soon Nanny and Roger came running into the room. Tears of happiness streamed down Nanny's face as she dusted off the little puppies.

"How did you get yourselves into this state?" she asked.

"Now that's a real mystery," said Roger. "I suppose we'll never know. Maybe I can write a song about it."

Perdita and Pongo looked around at their puppies. They would save their story for their grandchildren.

Anita counted the puppies. "Ninety-eight, ninety-nine. That makes one hundred and one, including Perdita and Pongo. What a family!!"

Everyone was delighted. Even Nanny, who was going to have to look after all those puppies.

Roger sat down at the piano and began to play. The puppies listened to the music. This was even better than TV!

Published by Gallery Books
A Division of W.H. Smith Publishers Inc.
112 Madison Avenue
New York, New York 10016.

Produced by
Twin Books
15 Sherwood Place
Greenwich, CT. 06830.

ISBN 0-8317-0020-3

Printed and bound in Spain

2 3 4 5 6 7 8 9 10